The
Heart
of a
GIANT

For Samuel, Nathan and Charlotte – *H.H.*

For my incredible Mum and Dad who taught me the magic of books,
and my Dave who believed I could make them – *A.W.*

BLOOMSBURY CHILDREN'S BOOKS
Bloomsbury Publishing Plc
50 Bedford Square, London WC1B 3DP, UK
29 Earlsfort Terrace, Dublin 2, Ireland

BLOOMSBURY, BLOOMSBURY CHILDREN'S BOOKS and the Diana logo are trademarks of Bloomsbury Publishing Plc

First published in Great Britain by Bloomsbury Publishing Plc

Text copyright © Hollie Hughes 2022
Illustrations copyright © Anna Wilson 2022

Hollie Hughes and Anna Wilson have asserted their rights under the Copyright, Designs and Patents Act, 1988,
to be identified as the Author and Illustrator of this work

A catalogue record for this book is available from the British Library

ISBN 978 1 4088 8055 5 (HB)
ISBN 978 1 4088 8056 2 (eBook)

1 3 5 7 9 10 8 6 4 2

Printed in China by Leo Paper Products, Heshan, Guangdong

MIX
Paper from
responsible sources
FSC® C020056

To find out more about our authors and books visit www.bloomsbury.com and sign up for our newsletters

The Heart of a GIANT

written by

Hollie Hughes

illustrated by

Anna Wilson

BLOOMSBURY
CHILDREN'S BOOKS

LONDON OXFORD NEW YORK NEW DELHI SYDNEY

There's a shape up in the hills,
where a giant's said to sleep,
beneath a grassy blanket,
on a bed of moss and peat.

There's a boy whose name is *Tom*,
whose mam has gone away,
but the hills are always there . . .

and he climbs them every day.

Tom lies upon the giant's chest, his ear pressed to the ground.
He listens for a HEARTBEAT,
and he's sure he hears it pound.

As he hugs the sleeping giant,
the earth begins to

Tom is tumbling,
falling down . . .

Tom finds his feet and holds his ground – he doesn't run away.
He thinks at first he'll turn and hide . . .

then **something** makes him **stay**.

For though the giant is **mighty**, with his eyes all burning wild,
it somehow seems to Tom that this great giant is just a **child**.

The giant's name is *Abram* –
he says *Tom* can call him *Abe* –
and in that special moment,
a new friendship is soon made.

Mammy Giant left *Abe* to nap a hundred years ago,
but now he's tired of waiting, and he quickly tells *Tom* so.

And though *Tom* knows his own mam cannot **ever** come back home,
he doesn't want his giant friend to also be **alone**.

Abe's mammy might need help, they think –
she may have lost her way.
So the two of them decide to search,
and set off straightaway.

Abe the giant picks *Tom* up
and sets him on his shoulder,
and off the new friends go,

over hill

and stream

and boulder.

They wander through a meadow
in a haze of butterflies,

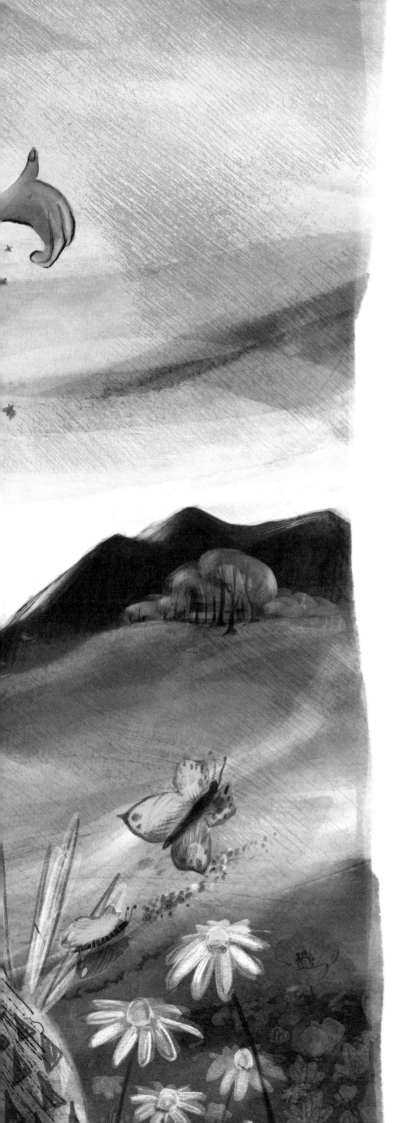

then come upon
an ancient wood . . .

. . . where PIXIE
magic lies!

Within a dark and earthy den, they rest by emerald pools,
to stop and watch the tiny folk
at work with picks and tools.

And for a time, the friends forget
what's led them to this place,
and they just enjoy the moment
in the magic wood's embrace.

But as they leave the woods behind,
there's coolness in the air.
They know that Mammy Giant
might still need their help out there.

By day and night they journey on
through lands of ice and snow,
where white bears growl, and great wolves howl,
and biting blizzards blow.

Their steps give way to nowhere,
and they're filled with cold and dread.
They must have walked a million miles
since *Abe* was safe in bed.

They're no longer feeling hopeful,
like they were when this began,
and *Abe* is doubting deeply
that they'll **ever** find his mam.

They've searched for her forever
          and have now looked **everywhere**,
      and he can't contain the howl of pain
          that shakes the land and air.

The giant
STOMPS
his mighty foot and
tears the ground apart.

And it opens up a CRATER . . .

like the hole inside his heart.

The peaks begin to CREAK and shift, and avalanches fall.
Tom knows he must act quickly to save anything at all.

But how can Tom stop a giant, with temper fiery wild?

How can he save
a CRASHING world
when he is just
a child?

Tom tells Abe to listen,
and believe in something TRUE –
that, even when someone is lost, they live inside of YOU.

This was what his mam had said
before they'd had to part,
that each of them would always be . . .

within the other's
HEART.

As *Abe* the giant wipes his eyes,
the sun begins to shine.

The hills of home are calling –
they've been gone
TOO LONG a time.

And when the well-known peaks and dales are finally in view,

it seems that someone even BIGGER might be back home too . . .

Mammy Giant has come at last, to wake her giant lad,
and *Abe* is beaming broadly now,
no longer feeling sad!

He tells his mam the story
of how *Tom* has made him strong,
and tried so hard to help him,
even with his own mam gone.

So, Mammy Giant smiles
and says that *Tom* is
just the best . . .

and surely has a GIANT heart
within his human chest.

And deep down in his GIANT heart,
Tom knows it's time for home.
For even though his mam has gone,
he doesn't live alone.

There are people there that love him,
and who he loves back too . . .

with the **heart** of a GIANT
that is steady, strong
and **true**.